·ONE· SATURDAY EVENING

BY Barbara Baker · PICTURES BY Kate Duke

Dutton Children's Books

DUTTON CHILDREN'S BOOKS
A division of Penguin Young Readers Group
Published by the Penguin Group
Penguin Group (USA) Inc., 375 Hudson Street, New York,
New York 10014, U.S.A. • Penguin Group (Canada), 90 Eglinton
Avenue East, Suite 700, Toronto, Ontario, Canada M4P 2Y3
(a division of Pearson Penguin Canada Inc.) • Penguin Books Ltd,
80 Strand, London WC2R 0RL, England • Penguin Ireland,
25 St Stephen's Green, Dublin 2, Ireland (a division of Penguin Books Ltd)
Penguin Group (Australia), 250 Camberwell Road, Camberwell, Victoria 3124,
Australia (a division of Pearson Australia Group Pty Ltd) • Penguin Books India Pvt Ltd,
11 Community Centre, Panchsheel Park, New Delhi—110 017, India • Penguin Group
(NZ), Cnr Airborne and Rosedale Roads, Albany, Auckland 1310, New Zealand (a division of
Pearson New Zealand Ltd) • Penguin Books (South Africa) (Pty) Ltd, 24 Sturdee Avenue,
Rosebank, Johannesburg 2196, South Africa • Penguin Books Ltd, Registered Offices:
80 Strand, London WC2R 0RL, England

LIBRARY OF CONGRESS CATALOGING-IN-PUBLICATION DATA
Baker, Barbara, date.
One Saturday evening/by Barbara Baker ; pictures by Kate Duke.—1st ed.
p. cm.
Summary: On a Saturday evening, the members of a bear family busy themselves
with cleaning up the kitchen, taking baths, and reading.
ISBN: 978-0-525-47103-5 (hardcover) [1. Family life—Fiction. 2. Bears—Fiction.]
I. Duke, Kate, ill. II. Title.
PZ7.B16922Om 2007 [E]—dc21
2006024785

Published in the United States by Dutton Children's Books,
a division of Penguin Young Readers Group
345 Hudson Street, New York, New York 10014
www.penguin.com/youngreaders

Designed by Jason Henry
Manufactured in China • First Edition
1 3 5 7 9 10 8 6 4 2

For Miriam
—B.A.B.

To Paddington, Pooh, and Little
—K.D.

CONTENTS

MAMA

One Saturday evening

everyone finished eating dinner.

"That was good," Mama said.

"But now I have

a lot of work to do."

Mama got up from the table.

She began to work.

First she washed all the dishes.

Then she washed the table.

Then she washed the floor.

Then she washed Jack.

"No!" said Jack.

"Yes," said Mama.

Papa came into the kitchen.

"It is nice and clean in here,"

he said.

"Yes, it is," said Mama.

"I washed all the dishes

and the table

and the floor

and Jack."

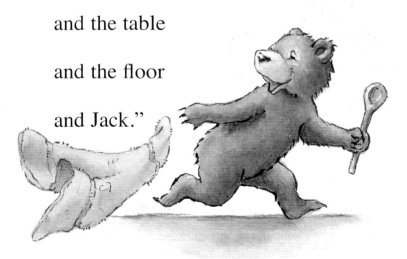

"Are you finished?" said Papa.

"No," said Mama.

"There is one more thing

I want to wash."

10

Mama went into the bathroom.

She closed the door.

She filled the tub

with warm water.

"Just right," she said.

Mama got into the bathtub.

She washed her hands

and her face

and her arms

and her feet.

Then she lay back in the warm water.

"Ahhh," said Mama.

"That feels good."

The bathroom was quiet

and peaceful.

Mama was happy.

Mama loved Saturday evenings.

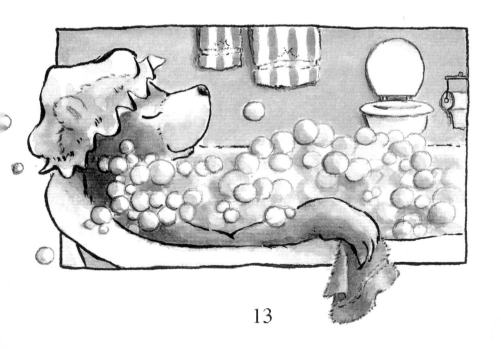

LILY

"I want to take a bath

all by myself," said Lily.

"But Lily," said Mama,

"you always take a bath

with Rose and Daisy."

"No more," said Lily.

"I am big now.

I can take a bath

all by myself."

Mama looked at the big bathtub.

She looked at Lily.

"Okay," said Mama.

Then Mama helped Lily

get into the tub.

"You can go now," said Lily.

So Mama left.

Lily was all by herself

in the big bathtub.

First she sat at one end of the tub.

Then she sat at the other end.

Then she sat in the middle.

She put her face in the water

and blew bubbles.

Then she played with

all of the bath toys.

Lily made waves in the water

with her hands.

"Lily," Mama called,

"are you done yet?"

"Almost," said Lily.

"But I need a little help."

Mama came back.

She helped Lily wash her face

and her arms

and her feet

and her back.

Then Mama helped Lily

out of the tub.

She gave Lily a big towel.

Lily dried her face and her hands.

Then Mama dried the rest of Lily.

"All done," said Mama.

Lily put on her pajamas.

"You did a good job," said Mama.

"Yes," said Lily.

"I am big now.

I like taking a bath *all* by myself."

ROSE

Rose loved bath time.

She liked to splash.

She liked to swim.

And she liked to sing

in a loud, loud voice.

"Rose," said Mama.

"Do you have to be so wild?"

"Wild, wild, *wild,*"

sang Rose.

Then Rose dumped a cup of water

on Daisy's head.

"Mama!" cried Daisy.

Mama helped Rose

out of the bathtub.

Water was everywhere.

Then Mama helped Rose dry off.

Rose ran to Papa.

"Look, Papa," she said.

"I am nice and clean."

Papa was reading a quiet book

to Jack.

"Shhh," said Papa.

"Jack is getting sleepy."

"I am not sleepy," said Rose.

"I am nice and clean

and wide-awake."

"I can see that," said Papa.

"Down," said Jack.

Now Jack was not sleepy.

Papa put Jack down.

Daisy and Lily came running.

"Grrrr," said Rose.

"I am a big, wild monster."

Soon everyone was running

and screaming.

"Rose," said Papa,

"you are too wild!"

Rose came over to Papa.

She got up on his lap.

"I am nice and clean, Papa,"

she said.

"Yes," said Papa.

"You smell as sweet as a rose."

"A wild rose," said Rose.

Lily and Daisy and Jack

were still playing.

"Read to me, Papa,"

said Rose.

So Papa read a quiet story

to his sweet, wild Rose.

"Mmm," said Rose. "Nice."

DAISY

Daisy was playing

with her baby doll.

Papa was reading a book

to Lily and Rose.

And Mama was putting

Jack to bed.

"No, no, NO!" cried Jack.

He was making a big fuss.

"*My* baby does not

make a big fuss," said Daisy.

"My baby is good."

31

Daisy sang a little song

to her baby.

"Now it is time for bed, baby,"

said Daisy.

Daisy put her baby doll's pajamas on.

Then she tucked her into

her little bed.

"Night, night," said Daisy.

The baby doll went right to sleep.

"Look, Papa," said Daisy.

"*My* baby is sleeping.

My baby is very good."

"Yes," said Papa.

"Now it is time for all of you

to go to bed."

"No, no, *no!*" called Jack.

Papa closed the book.

"I am not tired," said Lily.

"I am not tired," said Rose.

Papa looked at Daisy.

"No, no, no!" cried Daisy.

JACK

Jack was in his crib.

He was not happy.

"Up, up," he said.

"It is time to go to sleep, Jack,"

said Mama.

"No," said Jack. "Up."

Mama tucked Jack in.

She gave Jack a good-night kiss.

Then she left.

"Up, up," called Jack.

But Mama did not come back.

So Jack got busy.

He pushed.

He pulled.

He climbed.

And finally Jack was

up

and out

and down.

Now Jack was happy.

Later Papa came in

to give Jack

a good-night kiss.

"Oh, dear!" said Papa.

Jack was not in his crib.

Jack was under his crib.

He was asleep.

Papa picked him up.

He put him into his crib.

"Up," said Jack.

PAPA

Papa loved to read.

Lily and Rose and Daisy and Jack

were in bed.

Mama was making cocoa.

And Papa was reading

a good book.

"Someday," said Papa,

"I will write a book.

Someday…when I am not busy."

"You are not busy right now,"

said Mama.

"This would be a good time

for you to begin."

Mama got some paper and a pen.

She gave them to Papa.

Papa picked up the pen.

Once upon a time, he wrote.

Then he stopped.

"I do not know

what to write about," said Papa.

"I do," said Mama.

"You could write about wild animals."

"No," said Papa.

"Or you could write about monsters."

"No," said Papa.

"How about a ghost story?"

said Mama.

"No," said Papa.

"Your ideas are good," he said.

"But I have a better one."

Then Papa gave the paper and pen to Mama.

"This is my idea," he said.

"*You* can write a story.

And *I* will finish reading my book."

Papa poured some cocoa for Mama

and some cocoa for himself.

They sat down together.

Mama began to write.

Papa took a sip of his cocoa.

He opened his good book.

"Ahhh," said Papa.

Papa loved Saturday evenings.